THE HIDDEN HAND

By J.D. Maverick

The Hidden Hand
Copyright © 2025 J.D. Maverick
All rights reserved.

No part of this book may be reproduced, stored in a retrieval system, or transmitted in any form or by any means—electronic, mechanical, photocopying, recording, or otherwise—without the prior written permission of the author, except for brief quotes in reviews or articles.

This is a work of fiction. Any resemblance to actual persons, living or dead, or actual events is purely coincidental.

Published by J.D. Maverick
ISBN-13: 9798992813685

John F. Kennedy's Address Before the American Newspaper Publishers Association
Waldorf-Astoria Hotel, New York City
April 27, 1961

"For we are opposed around the world by a monolithic and ruthless conspiracy that relies primarily on covert means for expanding its sphere of influence—on infiltration instead of invasion, on subversion instead of elections, on intimidation instead of free choice, on guerrillas by night instead of armies by day. It is a system which has conscripted vast human and material resources into the building of a tightly knit, highly efficient machine that combines military, diplomatic, intelligence, economic, scientific and political operations. Its preparations are concealed, not published. Its mistakes are buried, not headlined. Its dissenters are silenced, not praised. No expenditure is questioned, no rumor is printed, no secret is revealed."

— John F. Kennedy (1917-1963)

TABLE OF CONTENTS

Chapter 1 The Architects Below 1

Chapter 2 The Divine Hand 8

Chapter 3 The Doctrine of Knowledge 13

Chapter 4 The Art of Illusion 19

Chapter 5 Beneath the Shimmering Veil 25

Chapter 6 Quiet Conformity 30

Chapter 7 The Price of Clarity 35

Chapter 8 The Breaking Point 39

Chapter 9 Extinguish the Flame 45

Chapter 10 A Spark in the Dark 51

Chapter 11 Shifting the Balance 55

Chapter 12 Through Enemy Gates 61

Chapter 13 The Other Side of Truth 67

CHAPTER 1
THE ARCHITECTS BELOW

Deep beneath the Earth's crust, there lay a city unlike any known to humanity. Erebos was its name, a sprawling metropolis of crystalline towers that shimmered like the inside of a diamond, suspended in an eternal ocean of darkness. The light from within these towers pulsed with an otherworldly glow, casting long, elegant shadows that seemed to stretch into infinity. Above, the heavens remained as they always had, a vast expanse of oblivion. Below, there was nothing but the hum of life, the constant flow of energy and thought that permeated the city of Erebos.

In the heart of this subterranean kingdom, the air was alive with activity. Floating archives, ethereal and translucent, drifted gently through the air. These were no ordinary libraries. Held aloft by magnetic fields, their contents were encoded in languages and symbols no human mind had ever comprehended. Their knowledge was infinite, and yet it remained out of reach for those above who believed themselves to be the only intelligent life on Earth. Erebos was the true cradle of civilization, the birthplace of knowledge and progress. The Erebites had developed technologies so advanced that they appeared to be little more than magic to anyone who had never been privy to their secrets. Seamless, invisible roads crisscrossed the city, carrying individuals swiftly to their destinations. Luminescent plants, thriving off pure energy, grew in elegant patterns, their colors shifting in harmony with the rhythms of the city. Every aspect of Erebos was a testament to the mastery of those who had built it, a civilization that had existed for millennia, hidden in the depths of the Earth.

To the Erebites, their city was more than just a home. It was a sanctuary. Theirs was a world of order, purpose, and absolute control. And they had lived in the shadows, unseen and unknown to the humans who walked upon the surface, for as long as they could remember. Their existence was carefully concealed. But while humanity above remained blissfully ignorant of their creators, the Erebites knew everything about them. They had watched the surface dwellers for centuries, even millennia, observing their every move. Their methods were subtle, indirect, but always effective. The Erebites had guided civilization from the shadows, nudging it along in secret—bending empires, orchestrating revolutions, and tweaking the course of history to ensure the survival of the human species. Their influence extended into every corner of human existence. They had shaped everything from politics to culture, from religion to war. It was not a matter of personal desire or ambition—it was simply a matter of necessity.

To the Erebites, humanity was a volatile, dangerous species—restless, ambitious, and prone to self-destruction. Left unchecked, humanity would have burned itself to ash long ago. The Erebites had seen the potential for destruction in the human race, the way their emotions and desires could spiral into chaos. It had happened before. They had seen the fall of empires, the rise of violence, the collapse of entire societies. Without their intervention, humanity would have doomed itself to extinction. And so, they had acted, guiding humanity's development from the shadows, shaping its history from afar. Their role was one of protection—not domination. The Erebites had not shaped humanity to rule over them, but to safeguard their existence. They had made sure that, despite their flaws, humanity would survive.

Religion had been their first tool. It was an ancient and effective strategy, one that had served the Erebites well for centuries. They whispered to prophets, carving commandments into stone, weaving myths that would steer entire civilizations toward obedience and control. The most powerful of kings and emperors, those who ruled vast kingdoms and empires, believed themselves chosen by the gods. They declared divine right as the foundation of their power, never once suspecting that the gods they revered were scholars of Erebos. These were not deities but men and women of incredible intellect, using their knowledge to shape human history and ensure the balance of power. It was a delicate operation, one that required the utmost care and discretion. The Erebites had carefully calibrated the balance of faith. It was all for the greater good, they believed.

As the centuries passed, the Erebites saw that religion alone was no longer enough to maintain control over humanity. Faith began to wane, especially as the surface world entered the age of reason. The development of science and philosophy threatened to unravel the foundation of human belief. Humanity's thirst for knowledge and progress had given rise to new ways of thinking, new ideas that were often incompatible with the ancient myths the Erebites had created. And so, they adapted. They shifted their methods. They turned to education.

Universities and scientific discoveries were allowed to flourish, but only within certain limits. The brightest minds of each era were carefully shepherded along their paths, guided away from dangerous ideas that could lead them too close to the truth. The Erebites made sure that no one ever came close to uncovering their existence. The most brilliant minds, those who might have discovered the truth about Erebos, were subtly redirected, their research subtly thwarted. A well-placed war, an unfortunate accident, or a purged library could erase the inconvenient facts that might lead to a dangerous discovery. The Erebites had become masters of control, bending not just religions but entire civilizations to their will.

In the modern age, the Erebites had perfected their methods. No longer did they need myths or censorship. They had something far more effective: algorithms. Media empires. Echo chambers. The world above had become a vast network of interconnected systems, each one feeding information into the next. The Erebites had learned how to manipulate the flow of information, twisting truth until it was no longer recognizable. Humanity, for all its seeming progress, had been lulled into a false sense of freedom. They believed they were making choices, discovering the truth for themselves, but in reality, their every thought, their every decision, had been carefully curated.

But now, a problem had emerged. A signal, faint at first, had begun to rise from the depths of the internet—an unexpected disturbance that caught the attention of the Erebites. It came in the form of a musician, Lysandra Kaelith, whose art had captivated millions. Known as a brilliant composer and virtuoso, her music had always been abstract and poetic, a reflection of the world around her. But in recent years, her works had taken a new turn.

Her latest compositions carried a hidden undertone—one that subtly questioned the very nature of reality. Her lyrics, once simple and melodic, now spoke of cryptic truths, veiled in metaphor, but unmistakable to those who listened closely. In her symphonies, strange patterns began to emerge—patterns that hinted at a deeper, secret history, one that could challenge the very foundations of everything the Erebites had worked to preserve.

Her music, though beautiful, was now filled with a quiet rebellion, a suggestion that the history humanity had been taught, the world they believed they understood, might be nothing more than an elaborate lie. The Erebites could feel the threat growing, though it was still distant, still veiled beneath layers of public admiration.

For now, they could only watch her rise, monitoring her every performance and interview. Yet, in the quiet spaces between the notes, they could sense the cracks forming in the carefully constructed narrative that had held the surface world together for centuries.

Not everyone in Erebos felt the same. Among the overseers, one stood out—Kosta, the son of Emperor Lorkan, the most powerful person in all of Erebos. His role was clear: observe, maintain, and protect. Raised from birth to uphold the Erebites' mission, he was a loyal servant of the system, unyielding in his belief that humanity needed their guidance. But as he watched Lysandra's work unfold on the screens before him, something inside him began to stir.

He had been trained to believe in the Erebites' cause, to believe that humanity's flaws required constant guidance. But now—now he wasn't so sure.

What if their methods had been flawed all along? What if, in their quest to protect humanity, they had stifled its potential instead of nurturing it? Kosta had watched the Erebites manipulate the course of history, and while the results had often prevented chaos, he couldn't help but wonder: had their actions truly been for the greater good? Or had they merely been playing God, dictating what humanity could and couldn't become?

His father, Emperor Lorkan, noticed his hesitation. He was a man of absolute conviction, unyielding in his belief that the Erebites' rule over humanity was for their own good. He had seen the chaos that would arise if humanity were left to its own devices. And he would not allow anyone to jeopardize the delicate balance they had created.

"You're thinking too much, Kosta," Lorkan said, his voice icy as he reviewed the latest updates on Lysandra. "The human mind is volatile, dangerous. It needs our guidance. You know this."

Kosta didn't answer immediately. His gaze remained fixed on the screen, where Lysandra's image appeared—still a figure of defiance, her boldness unbroken by the weight of the world around her. It was almost admirable, a glimpse of something rare. But he couldn't help but think it was also dangerously reckless.

"I do," he replied, his voice calm but his mind swirling. "But what if we've been wrong about what they need?"

Lorkan's eyes flickered with a warning. "Do not forget your place, Kosta. Erebos's mission is not to question. It is to protect. If Lysandra continues her rebellion, we will act swiftly. Do not make the mistake of sympathizing with her."

But Kosta couldn't shake the thought that had taken root in his mind. He had always believed in the Erebites' cause, but now... now, he wasn't so sure. What if their intervention had been too much? Had their control been the reason humanity had never risen to its full potential?

As the Erebites watched from the shadows, one question continued to gnaw at Kosta' mind: Had they been good shepherds all these years? Or had their influence, their manipulation, suppressed humanity's true path?

CHAPTER 2
THE DIVINE HAND

For the Erebites, control of religion was not merely a governing tool—it was an intricate art form. They wielded it with precision, shaping the very nature of human belief. Religion was their first and most powerful means of manipulating the human race, a subtle, invisible force that had guided civilizations from their earliest steps. They did not just control worship or rituals; they directed the way humanity thought, felt, and believed. It was vital to their survival, more crucial than anything else.

In the earliest days, when humans were still emerging from the primordial chaos, the Erebites watched from their hidden realm beneath the Earth. They saw the potential for great upheaval and destruction, recognizing humanity's insatiable need for meaning. They knew the primitive beliefs taking shape were unformed and fraught with superstition, capable of spiraling out of control. Left unchecked, the human thirst for understanding could ravage the world. So, the Erebites intervened.

They whispered to the prophets, guiding their visions with careful precision, urging them to proclaim divine messages that would align with the Erebites' objectives. These myths and visions became the bedrock of the earliest civilizations, shaping the political, cultural, and social landscapes. Kings and emperors rose not on merit or strength, but by divine mandate. Guided by the Erebites, their power became absolute and unquestionable. They had crafted a model—a model of divine rulers who would never be challenged, for who could question the will of the gods?

In ancient Sumer, as the first cities blossomed from the fertile rivers of the Tigris and Euphrates, the Erebites whispered to the high priests. They planted the idea that the gods resided in a distant realm above the mortal world, unreachable, untouchable. In truth, the gods were not in the heavens but were idols created beneath the Earth, in the depths of Erebos. The Erebites chose their human representatives, shaping the course of history and civilization itself from the shadows, molding human belief.

Enheduanna, the High Priestess of Nanna, was one of the most influential figures to hear their call. As the daughter of Sargon of Akkad, she held immense power, not just as a political figure but as a religious leader. The hymns she composed—songs of devotion to Inanna and other gods—were not merely acts of faith, but carefully guided messages implanted by the Erebites. Her words shaped the spiritual consciousness of Sumer, binding the people to their deities with an intensity never before seen. She believed her visions came from the divine, but in truth, they were the work of the Erebites, subtly guiding her mind and her purpose.

Through Enheduanna, the Erebites ensured that religious doctrine would intertwine with governance, solidifying their grip on human civilization. Her hymns reinforced the idea of divine order, the sacredness of kingship, and the necessity of submission to higher forces. She was their instrument, unknowingly weaving a belief system that would endure for millennia. The Erebites did not need to appear in person. They understood that the true power lay in ideas and belief, not in physical presence. They understood that if they could bend the minds of humanity to their will, they could control the world. They had created a structure—a foundation on which empires and cultures would be built.

As the Crusades began to shape the medieval world, the Erebites saw an opportunity unlike any before. The growing tension between Christianity and Islam became the perfect battleground for their influence. Two figures emerged as pawns in their grand design: Pope Urban II and Sultan Malik-Shah I. Both men, powerful in their own right, were driven by the forces that the Erebites had carefully set into motion.

Pope Urban II, with his impassioned call to arms at the Council of Clermont, set forth a holy war that would galvanize Europe. The idea of reclaiming the Holy Land was not merely a military endeavor; it was the ultimate reinforcement of divine authority.

At the same time, across the Islamic world, Sultan Malik-Shah I was expanding the power of the Seljuk Empire, unifying vast territories under his rule. His governance saw the flourishing of Islamic scholarship and culture.

The Erebites whispered to both the leaders of the Islamic world and the Christian world, guiding their direction, ensuring that Islam and Christianity would thrive, and never wane. By strengthening both faiths, they guaranteed a perpetual clash of civilizations. Two religions, each believing itself to be the sole bearer of truth, locked in an endless cycle of war and reconciliation. And through it all, the Erebites maintained their hold, ensuring that humanity remained distracted, never questioning the deeper forces at play.

As the secular age began to take hold, the Erebites adapted once more. Though religion was no longer the sole guiding force, belief itself had not disappeared. It simply transformed into new forms. Nationalism became the new faith, and the Erebites, ever vigilant, whispered in the ears of rulers. They helped shape ideologies that bound people to their countries, their flags, and their leaders—equally divine in their own right.

The Erebites knew better than anyone that belief could be twisted and molded into any form. Whether through gods, kings, or political ideologies, if a person believed that their actions were the result of divine will, they would follow without question. If an entire nation believed it was destined for greatness, it would march forward without considering the consequences. Belief was a tool, a weapon to control and inspire, to unite and divide. It was the key to humanity's spirit.

As the centuries turned to millennia, the Erebites' influence over religion grew so deeply embedded that no one questioned it. Religion had become invisible, woven into the fabric of daily life. No one realized that their belief systems, from the gods of ancient Egypt to the political ideologies of modern times, had all been subtly shaped by the Erebites.

But now, with Lysandra Kaelith threatening to expose the truth, the Erebites faced a new challenge. What would happen if humanity discovered that their faith—whether in gods, kings, or ideologies—had always been a tool of manipulation? Would they collapse in disillusionment, or would they cling to their beliefs with even more fervor? For the Erebites, the stakes had never been higher. The foundation of control they had spent millennia building was at risk of being shattered. The consequences of exposure could be catastrophic, and they wondered if the control they had so carefully orchestrated would unravel in ways they had never anticipated.

And Kosta, the son of Emperor Lorkan, once a proud architect of the Erebites' plans, began to question everything. Was it worth it? Had they gone too far? The weight of their manipulation was becoming unbearable.

CHAPTER 3
THE DOCTRINE OF KNOWLEDGE

The Erebites had long understood the power of knowledge. Information was not merely power—it was the foundation of control. By shaping education, they could direct the course of human thought, creating minds that would never question the world they were born into. To them, education was more than the dissemination of facts; it was the art of crafting reality itself. Knowledge was not simply passed down—it was carefully constructed, edited, and curated to reinforce the systems of control that the Erebites had designed. Every textbook, every lecture, every lesson was another brick in a wall built to confine human curiosity.

From the earliest days of human civilization, the Erebites had carefully curated what humanity learned. The first signs of written language were manipulated with subtlety. In the ancient libraries of Alexandria, where scholars once sought the wisdom of the ancient world, the Erebites had planted their agents. Scholars, though brilliant, had never been allowed to come close to understanding the true nature of the universe—how deep beneath the Earth, in the dark recesses of Erebos, knowledge stretched far beyond the reach of even their most enlightened minds. The Erebites understood that knowledge was both a tool and a weapon; if wielded properly, it could shape the future of humanity.

The Erebites did not need to directly control every text or manuscript. Instead, they sowed seeds of doubt and destruction into the institutions of learning. When they wanted a discovery suppressed, a library would burn. When they wanted a theory to fade into obscurity, they simply allowed it to be ridiculed or discredited. Throughout history, the brightest minds of each generation had been manipulated into pursuing safe, inconsequential knowledge, their work ultimately directed toward advancements that would never challenge Erebos's supremacy. Scholars who began to ask dangerous questions were subtly sidelined, their inquiries deemed irrelevant or impractical. Those who discovered truths that threatened the carefully constructed narrative of human existence found their works forgotten or condemned.

One of the most memorable examples of this manipulation occurred during the Renaissance, a period of great intellectual awakening. It was a time when humanity seemed poised to challenge the boundaries of knowledge and break free from the constraints of religion and superstition. But the Erebites had already anticipated this. They knew that the Renaissance was a dangerous time, a time when human ingenuity and curiosity could spark revolutions that threatened the very fabric of control they had woven for millennia.

In Florence, the historian and political thinker, Francesco Guicciardini, had started to uncover patterns in governance and power that hinted at deeper, unseen forces shaping human history. His writings, full of sharp political analysis, began to question the mechanisms of authority and control in ways that made the Erebites uneasy. If these ideas took root, they could inspire a new era of political self-awareness that might unravel everything the Erebites had carefully built. Questions about the true nature of governance, the origins of power, and the hidden hands that shaped history were dangerous ideas the Erebites could not afford to let flourish.

So, they intervened.

Through their influence over the Medici family and other powerful patrons of the Renaissance, the Erebites ensured that Guicciardini's more radical thoughts remained obscure. They directed attention toward more conventional historical narratives, emphasizing themes of stability, divine right, and inevitable cycles of power. His insights, though brilliant, were subtly redirected into safer academic discussions, preventing them from inspiring any real challenge to the status quo. The very institutions that celebrated historical inquiry ensured that the most dangerous ideas remained hidden in plain sight.

Centuries later, in the 20th century, the Erebites faced another threat, this time from the realm of historical scholarship. The historian David Irving, though a controversial figure, had stumbled upon documents and narratives that contradicted the accepted version of history in unsettling ways. His research suggested that history, as humanity understood it, had been meticulously shaped and edited. Though Irving himself became a divisive figure, the mere fact that he had begun to challenge entrenched historical narratives posed a potential risk to the Erebites' carefully maintained control over knowledge.

Again, they intervened.

Rather than outright silencing him, they allowed his work to become entangled in controversy and disrepute. They ensured that his findings, regardless of merit, were seen as extreme, making it easy to dismiss his research as the work of a fringe thinker. By turning him into a polarizing figure, they ensured that serious scholars would hesitate to engage with any potentially uncomfortable truths hidden within his work. The Erebites understood that suppression was not always necessary—sometimes, all that was needed was to taint the messenger, making the message too toxic to be considered rationally.

Even as the world moved into the modern era, the Erebites adapted their methods to suit the changing landscape. The rise of global education systems, universities, and academic institutions was welcomed—but only as long as these institutions adhered to the curriculum that the Erebites had set. Through carefully orchestrated alliances, they ensured that the brightest minds in every field were guided by invisible hands. Academic freedom was an illusion, a carefully constructed narrative that allowed the Erebites to maintain control. The Erebites had created a new form of education, one that seemed open and democratic, but was in fact another system designed to keep humanity in check.

For decades, universities operated under the illusion of independence, but their funding and research were often directed by Erebites interests. Scholars were encouraged to pursue studies that benefited humanity on a superficial level—advances in medicine, technology, and agriculture. However, any work that threatened to uncover the truth of the world, to reveal the existence of Erebos or challenge their position as silent guardians of humanity, was quashed. The Erebites were careful not to stifle all progress. They allowed for scientific advances, but they made sure those advances never questioned the core assumptions that kept their control intact. Innovations that were dangerous—those that might lead humanity closer to understanding their true history or purpose—were suppressed, dismissed as unimportant, or buried beneath layers of bureaucracy and doubt.

The rise of artificial intelligence and digital networks in the modern age presented a new challenge for the Erebites. In the beginning, they had embraced these new technologies as tools for advancing their control. They guided the development of the internet, shaping it into a vast, interconnected web of information. They saw the potential for controlling information at a scale they had never before imagined. The internet became another tool for ensuring that humanity's access to knowledge remained limited and controlled. But as humanity began to develop its own methods for searching for knowledge, the Erebites saw the potential for something far more dangerous. It was only a matter of time before someone stumbled upon the truth—someone like Lysandra Kaelith, whose unquenchable thirst for truth was now threatening to expose the Erebites' influence.

Lysandra Kaelith, a renowned musician and cultural icon, had used her fame and global platform to dig deeper into history's hidden truths. What began as an exploration of sound and soul had turned into a personal quest to uncover the secrets that had been buried for centuries. Her passion for discovery led her to challenge the very narratives that had shaped humanity's understanding of the world. Though not an academic by training, her findings were reverberating through intellectual circles, and more people were starting to listen.

Her research, shared through books, interviews, and performances, was becoming a movement—a collective awakening to the layers of history the Erebites had kept hidden. And now, with every new revelation, the Erebites found themselves facing a growing threat.

For the first time in centuries, someone was on the verge of unraveling the true nature of their existence. And for the Erebites, that was a risk they could not afford to let unfold.

CHAPTER 4
THE ART OF ILLUSION

The Erebites had long understood that control was not just about keeping humanity physically confined or ideologically subjugated. No, the most powerful form of control came from controlling perception. Through the careful orchestration of propaganda, they had learned how to shape the very reality that humans believed they were living in. The surface world, with its swirling politics and global conflicts, was but a stage—a grand illusion designed to keep the masses occupied, entertained, and obedient. The true manipulators worked in the shadows, controlling the story that the world believed, and that story was carefully constructed to maintain their influence.

It all began in the early days of mass communication, when the Erebites recognized the potential of the printing press. In the 15th century, as books and pamphlets began to circulate in Europe, the Erebites saw that the flow of information could be directed, altered, or entirely fabricated. While others focused on the potential of books to spread knowledge, the Erebites understood that it was not knowledge that could reshape the world, but stories. The narratives they created would rewrite history, frame the present, and define the future. History was not a fixed set of facts; itced altogether.

With the rise of the printing press, the Erebites began to manipulate this emerging medium. They recognized that the power of a story, when crafted correctly, could change the course of nations. Through strategically placed pamphlets, books, and newspapers, the Erebites could guide the thoughts of entire populations. The world's perception of what was true or false, right or wrong, was shaped not by unbiased facts, but by the stories that were told. The Erebites understood that truth was a malleable concept—it was not something objective, but something that could be shaped to suit their goals.

By the 20th century, their ability to craft and control narratives had reached new heights with the invention of radio, television, and, eventually, the internet. With each new medium, the Erebites refined their techniques, expanding their reach, and tightening their grip. They knew that in the modern world, the media would become their most powerful weapon. It wasn't enough to control governments or institutions—they had to control the narrative. And in the 20th century, they had the tools to do so more effectively than ever before.

As television took hold of the world, the Erebites knew that a new, more powerful tool had arrived. People no longer had to read stories in newspapers or books—they could watch them unfold before their eyes. And through the screens, the Erebites could implant ideas, shape opinions, and build entire realities. Television became the perfect medium for their purposes. The moving image, combined with sound, had an unparalleled ability to capture attention, stir emotion, and plant subtle suggestions into the subconscious of the viewer.

Television shows, advertisements, and political speeches were no longer simply forms of entertainment or communication—they were vehicles for ideological control. The Erebites knew that the human mind, captivated by moving images and carefully chosen words, was far more malleable than it had ever been before. Through carefully designed programs, commercials, and news broadcasts, they could shape public perception on an unimaginable scale. They could craft the images of heroes and villains, decide what was acceptable and what was taboo, and subtly enforce the narratives they wished to dominate.

In America, during the Cold War, the Erebites ensured that the narrative of democracy and freedom was entrenched in the hearts of the people. They used the fear of communism to unite the population under a common banner. The Cold War was not merely a battle between two ideologies; it was a carefully orchestrated stage play designed to keep humanity in a constant state of tension, never allowing them to focus on the true players behind the curtain. In the eyes of the public, the threat of communism was real, but it was also convenient—a perfect distraction from the far more insidious forces pulling the strings behind the scenes.

Through every conflict, every political shift, the Erebites guided the stories that would be told. They worked through leaders and influencers, but always from the shadows. Every protest, every revolution, every shift in power was watched, and when necessary, nudged in the right direction. If the Erebites wanted to ensure that a particular leader remained in power, they helped create a narrative that painted the opposition as dangerous, unpatriotic, or foolish. If they wanted to remove a leader who had become a threat to the status quo, they simply flooded the media with scandal, controversy, and dissent. The rise and fall of political leaders was not always the result of public opinion or democratic process—it was the result of a well-crafted narrative.

The rise of the internet in the late 20th and early 21st centuries presented a new challenge for the Erebites. The sheer volume of information now available to the world was overwhelming, and the speed at which it spread made traditional methods of control more difficult. But the Erebites were not deterred. Instead, they adapted their methods.

Through algorithms, social media platforms, and digital manipulation, the Erebites refined their approach. They didn't need to control every piece of content. Instead, they controlled the flow of content. They guided what would go viral, what would trend, and what would be ignored. The internet became a vast ocean of information, but the Erebites were the unseen currents that directed its flow. By controlling algorithms and trends, they could elevate specific voices and suppress others. They could promote divisive narratives and stoke conflicts, while silencing moderates and truth-seekers.

They created echo chambers, online communities that reinforced specific narratives and ideologies. If they wanted to stoke division, they flooded social media with incendiary content, amplifying the voices of extremists while silencing moderates. If they wanted to create a sense of urgency or fear, they used viral campaigns to spread misinformation, crafting fake news stories that sowed chaos and confusion. In this new digital age, the Erebites had mastered the art of controlling perception in ways that no one could have imagined in previous eras.

The Erebites had always understood that humans, in the end, were creatures of emotion. Facts and reason were secondary to feelings—fear, anger, hope, and desire. These emotions could be manipulated with precision, and through them, the Erebites shaped the course of history. The people above never knew the truth. They never questioned the systems they lived under, because the stories they were told had been carefully crafted to fit their expectations. What they believed was reality, but it was nothing more than an illusion, one designed by the Erebites to maintain their control.

And now, in the age of Lysandra Kaelith, the Erebites faced a new kind of challenge. Her fame had catapulted her into the spotlight, and with it, a growing ability to reveal the hidden truths that the Erebites had so carefully obscured. They knew her influence was a threat, and they would need to act quickly to silence her before her revelations could shatter their carefully constructed world.

The Erebites had built their empire on the art of illusion. And as the modern world entered its most volatile age, they were ready to craft a new narrative—one that would ensure the continued dominance of their hidden empire, no matter the cost.

CHAPTER 5
BENEATH THE SHIMMERING VEIL

Kosta stood at the edge of the crystalline bridge, his gaze following the lattices of pulsing light that mapped the city below. Erebos unfolded beneath him, a geometric sprawl of precision and symmetry. Towers of translucent crystal pierced the sky, their angular surfaces refracting the cold, sapphire glow emanating from the city's core. Floating structures drifted along fixed trajectories, guided by unseen forces, their motion synchronized with the slow, rhythmic pulse that throbbed through the very fabric of Erebos.

The city was a paradox—a marvel of perfect order wrapped around a core of suffocating control. To the untrained eye, it was utopia—a seamless fusion of technology and intellect, where every need was met before desire could form. But beneath its shimmering surface lay an ever-watchful presence, subtle yet inescapable.

The city did not flow with water or earth but with liquid light—currents of white and indigo energy that twisted through the city. They shifted in deliberate, preordained patterns, rerouting themselves according to the unseen directives of the Core. No one walked in Erebos. Its citizens glided along the illuminated streams, their steps barely disturbing the charged air. To exist in Erebos was to surrender the body to the city's rhythm—an offering to the machine that governed them all.

Kosta had grown up in Erebos, and he had seen it evolve, but every time he traversed through the city, the same awe stirred within him. Standing tall, with sharp features and light hazel brown eyes, Kosta was a reflection of the city around him—graceful, yet charged with quiet intensity. His dark hair, slightly tousled in soft waves, framed a face that conveyed both thoughtfulness and purpose. His movements were fluid and deliberate, each step guided by the pulse of the city itself. He wore sleek, deep blue and silver garments that allowed him to glide effortlessly through the shimmering pathways, blending seamlessly into the environment that had shaped him.

The architecture of Erebos was otherworldly—towers spiraling upward like the twisted fingers of ancient gods, their surfaces smooth and reflective, like glass but stronger than any stone. The light within each structure pulsed with a rhythm that matched the heartbeat of the city. It was as if the city itself was breathing, alive with energy and thought, its very existence an extension of the Erebites' will.

Kosta's role, like every Erebite before him, was to maintain the balance. He was a guardian, a protector of the secrets that lay buried beneath Erebos's gleaming surface. He had been trained from a young age to understand the intricacies of Erebites society—to know where every system, every structure, every piece of information belonged. His mission was simple: observe, ensure compliance, and, when necessary, intervene. For most Erebites, that was enough. The city was perfect. Humanity, though flawed and volatile, was safe because of the Erebites' guidance. It was a duty Kosta had accepted with pride—until now.

The air was thick with knowledge, with the weight of centuries of history and wisdom. Floating alongside Kosta were the archives—those ethereal, transparent orbs that contained all the accumulated knowledge of the Erebites. They hung in the air like fragile phantoms, transmitting their encoded secrets directly into the minds of those permitted to understand them. The knowledge within these archives was limitless—an eternal record of progress, invention, and discovery. To the Erebites, the pursuit of knowledge was not a goal—it was a way of life. It was how they had built Erebos, and it was how they would preserve it for as long as they could.

But knowledge was a double-edged sword. The more Kosta learned of the past, the more uneasy he became. The Erebites had watched over humanity for generations, subtly guiding them, influencing their path without direct interference. It was the foundation of their rule—control without oppression, guidance without force. Or so they believed.

As he reached the central hub of the city, the energy around him pulsed with renewed intensity. Above him, the massive towers stretched into the void, their crystal surfaces reflecting the glow of the central energy core. The air buzzed with the hum of activity, with the constant movement of Erebites citizens, each one focused on their tasks, each one a cog in the vast machinery that kept the city running. It was a harmonious existence, a perfect balance.

And yet, Kosta couldn't shake the feeling that something was wrong. He had spent his entire life within the confines of Erebos, and yet the more he witnessed, the more he questioned the system that governed their lives. He had always accepted the idea that the Erebites' control over humanity was necessary—that their subtle guidance kept the human race from descending into chaos. But now, as he watched the silent march of Erebos's citizens, all absorbed in their work, a thought crept into his mind: Had they truly been benevolent? Had they acted in humanity's best interest, or had they merely ensured their continued dominion over them?

Kosta was not one to voice his doubts. He had learned long ago that to question was to risk being labeled as weak, as unreliable. He had learned to push his thoughts aside, to follow the path laid before him without hesitation. But now, with Lysandra Kaelith looming in the background, he found it harder and harder to ignore the gnawing sense of unrest that had taken root in his heart.

The Erebites had never tolerated dissent—especially from someone like her. A threat to their authority, to their carefully crafted balance. What would they do with her?

Kosta knew their ways. They didn't hesitate when it came to eliminating what they saw as disorder. But was it ultimately the best choice? Would the world truly be better off without Kysandra Kaelith or was it just convenient for the Erebites if she was?

The question was dangerous. It was a thought that could unravel everything he had ever believed in. He tried to push it aside, to focus on his duty. But as he stood in the heart of the city, surrounded by the hum of Erebites life, the question lingered in his mind like an unsolvable riddle.

Kosta turned away from the central hub and made his way toward the council chambers. His father, Emperor Lorkan, would be waiting for him. The stern face of the Emperor was a constant reminder of the Erebites' resolve. A towering figure, his broad shoulders and salt-and-pepper hair exuded authority. His gaze was sharp, his presence commanding. It was a face that had been molded to ensure obedience, to remind Kosta that their family's duty came before all else.

As Kosta moved through the city, his mind wandered back to the question that had taken root within him. Had the Erebites steered humanity in the right direction? Had they truly served humanity, or had they simply become keepers of a fragile order that, perhaps, no longer served the greater good?

CHAPTER 6
QUIET CONFORMITY

The United States, in the shadow of its towering cities and endless stretches of suburban sprawl, appeared to be the epitome of prosperity and freedom. To those who dwelt in the above, it was a place of opportunity, success, and unwavering security. The world, as they saw it, was a well-oiled machine. Everything had its place, and every person had their role. The streets were lined with pristine buildings, gleaming cars, and neatly manicured lawns. The hustle of daily life seemed to pulse with an almost mechanical precision.

But underneath it all, there was an unseen force guiding every action, every thought, and every decision. Fear.

Fear didn't always roar. Sometimes, it whispered. It slithered into the minds of the people above, creeping along their thoughts, infecting their judgments. It existed in the unspoken rules of their society. People were afraid to ask the wrong questions, to seek out the truth, for fear of what might happen if they dug too deep. Those who questioned the system, the ones who dared to challenge the comfortable lies, were not seen as brave or inquisitive—they were seen as a threat.

At the local café, the usual hum of conversation filled the air. It was a warm morning, with the sun filtering through the tall windows, casting soft light on the polished wooden tables. The coffee shop was filled with the kind of people who had learned to live in the comfort of certainty. They discussed the mundane—their work, their families, their vacations—but always with an edge of something darker lingering in their words. A subtle tension that could be felt but never fully addressed.

"I heard about that new security measure they're rolling out across the city," said Frank, a man in his late 40s, his business suit slightly wrinkled as he sat down next to his colleague. "You know, the one with the facial recognition cameras?"

"Yeah, they've been talking about it for weeks," Lisa, his colleague, replied, glancing nervously over her shoulder as if expecting someone to overhear. "It's supposed to make things safer, right? They said it's for our own protection."

Frank laughed, a hollow sound that didn't reach his eyes. "Sure. 'For our protection.' I mean, I guess I'm not complaining. I've got nothing to hide."

Lisa nodded quickly, her smile forced. "Exactly. Nothing to hide. I'm all for it if it keeps us safe. You know, with all the unrest happening elsewhere in the world… It just makes sense."

"Yeah, it's crazy what's happening out there. But we're lucky. We've got it made here, right?" Frank leaned back in his chair, trying to sound more assured than he felt. "We've got our jobs, our homes, our little slice of heaven. All the chaos out there doesn't affect us." He paused, glancing at the television mounted on the café wall. The screen flashed with an announcement about the latest foreign conflict. "Anyway, can't be too careful. If you ask me, it's just about time we did this."

Lisa's eyes darted nervously to the screen. "Yeah… I mean, I've been hearing rumors… about people who… you know… say things they shouldn't. They've been disappearing."

Frank's face tightened for a moment, but then he quickly dismissed it with a soft chuckle. "Rumors. People always talk. It's not like they're going to come for us. We're good people. We follow the rules."

Lisa wasn't convinced. "I don't know… I've been hearing a lot about these 'infiltrators,' people trying to mess with the system. You think the authorities are really watching for our own good? Or is it… something else?"

Frank's gaze flickered around the room again. The bright fluorescent lights hummed overhead. He leaned forward, lowering his voice, though there was no one in earshot. "I don't want to think about it. If people want to stir things up, they can deal with the consequences. We've got enough to worry about as it is. Let's just keep our heads down and do our work."

Lisa's frown deepened, but she didn't press the matter further. It was always better not to ask too many questions. Frank was right—why rock the boat? Everything was fine. The system worked. It had to. There was nothing more to it.

A little further down the street, in a pristine office building, another group of people sat around a conference table. They were dressed in the sharp suits of corporate America, their faces composed but tired from the long hours of work. The conversation was all about the latest quarterly earnings report, the company's new marketing strategies, and how to optimize efficiency. The glow of the monitors and the endless flow of data seemed to feed into the illusion of control.

"Did you see the new social media trend? Some of these 'independent thinkers' are really starting to get traction online," one of the executives, Rachel, said with a raised brow. "It's scary. They're starting to ask questions, questioning everything. Why are things the way they are?"

"Isn't that always the case?" laughed Tim, sitting across from her. "People just love to stir up trouble. But they don't know how things really work. It's a well-oiled system. Everyone has their place. Why fix something that isn't broken?"

Rachel hesitated, taking a sip of her coffee. "True. But you know, it's getting harder to shut them down. The internet, the way things spread so fast… It's harder to control it all. Have you seen the posts about the so-called 'Erebite conspiracy'?"

Tim smirked. "Yes. Let them have their fun. I'm not worried. People like to complain. But at the end of the day, they are wasting their energy. Eventually, they'll just keep doing what they always do—consume, buy, and go along with the flow. Just like the rest of us. The system takes care of itself."

Rachel wasn't entirely convinced. "Maybe. But what if they're right? What if there's something bigger going on that we're not seeing?"

Tim laughed again, his voice laced with a touch of condescension. "Come on, Rachel. We've worked in this industry long enough to know better. You really think the system would let something 'bigger' happen? People want to believe in conspiracies because it makes them feel important. Makes them feel like they're in control. But trust me, they're not."

CHAPTER 7
PRICE OF CLARITY

Lysandra Kaelith stood alone in the quiet of her penthouse, the city sprawling beneath her in glittering contrast to the shadows that clung to the edges of her soul. The skyscrapers outside pulsed with artificial life, a dazzling façade of progress and prosperity. But to Lysandra, it was nothing more than a carefully orchestrated illusion. A comforting lie to keep the world blind. And once, she had been just as blind.

Tall and statuesque, Lysandra possessed an ethereal beauty that made her unforgettable. Her long waves of obsidian hair cascaded down her back like flowing ink, framing a face that was both delicate and commanding. Her skin, pale and flawless, seemed to glow under any light, an otherworldly radiance that only added to her mystique. But it was her eyes—wide, dark, and endlessly deep—that captivated most. They held a hypnotic quality, an unreadable depth that drew people in, making them forget their own thoughts, their own troubles. To the world, she was mesmerizing, untouchable. But to herself, she was simply a woman trapped in a reality that was never her own.

She had lived in that illusion, bathed in its adoration, its applause. She had believed in the sanctity of her art, convinced that music could heal, that it could elevate the human spirit. But all of that had crumbled the night her brother, Alric, died.

She closed her eyes, but the memory of that night was a wound that refused to fade. Alric had been the only one who truly saw her, who understood the burden she carried. He had been her anchor, her only tether to something real in a world of artifice.

The official story had been simple: an accident. A tragic overdose, the headlines had read. Another young man lost to recklessness, another cautionary tale. But Lysandra knew better. Alric had never touched a substance in his life. He had been careful, paranoid even, always whispering to her about the things he had begun to uncover—the cracks in the world's perfect veneer, the strings being pulled in the dark.

The night before his death, he had come to her in a panic, eyes wild, his voice barely above a whisper.

"They know I've been digging," he had said. "Lys, you have to be careful. Your music—it's not just entertainment. It's part of it. It's part of their design."

She had laughed then, thinking it was just another one of his theories. "Alric, you sound insane. Who are 'they'?"

His hands had gripped her shoulders, tight enough to hurt. "The Erebites, Lys. They're real. And they're watching you. They're using you."

She had shoved him away, irritation bubbling to the surface. "You need to stop this. You're scaring yourself."

He had stared at her, something breaking behind his eyes. "You don't see it yet," he had murmured. "But you will."

The next day, he was dead.

Lysandra had tried to believe the lie at first. It was easier to accept the accident than to entertain the horrible possibility that someone had silenced him. But grief had a way of sharpening perception. The inconsistencies gnawed at her—the missing security footage, the coroner's vague report, the way everyone seemed too eager to move on. And then there were his notes, hidden in his apartment, filled with frantic scribbles about subliminal frequencies, control mechanisms woven into entertainment, whispers of an ancient order that shaped reality itself.

The more she read, the more the world around her began to unravel. The glamour, the adoration—it was all a cage. And she was its most gilded prisoner.

Now, standing at the window, she traced a finger against the glass, watching the city pulse below her. How many others had died for knowing too much? How many had tried to fight back and been erased, forgotten? Alric had been right. She had been blind. But now she saw the truth, and it burned within her like a curse.

A knock at the door pulled her back. She turned, schooling her expression into something composed. When she opened it, Naomi, her manager, stood there, all false brightness and calculated charm.

"We need to go over the setlist for tonight," Naomi said. "The show is going to be huge."

Lysandra nodded. "Of course."

But as Naomi spoke, Lysandra's mind drifted. The stage, the lights, the adoration—it was all part of the illusion. And she was done playing her part.

Her voice, her music, had power. But perhaps it was time to use that power for something real.

For Alric.

For the truth.

And if it cost her everything?

So be it.

CHAPTER 8
BREAKING POINT

The stage was set. The lights had dimmed, and the air was thick with anticipation. Lysandra Kaelith stood backstage, her fingers trembling slightly as they brushed over the ivory keys of her piano. Tonight was supposed to be another performance, another night of glamour, applause, and adoration. Another night where she would be the perfect image—the star that the world loved, the voice that soothed the masses.

But tonight was different. Tonight, something inside her stirred, something more than the music, more than the roles she had played for so long. It was a quiet defiance, an awakening that had been building in her heart for months. The words were already forming in her mind—cryptic, unsettling, but the truth nonetheless. She wasn't sure what would happen when she spoke them, but she knew she couldn't go on pretending anymore.

The curtains parted with a soft swoosh, and the blinding lights hit her. The crowd erupted in applause, a sea of faces gazing up at her with adoration. The familiar warmth of the spotlight wrapped around her like a blanket, comforting and stifling at once. Lysandra smiled, her practiced grin, her flawless mask. But inside, she was trembling.

The band began playing the opening chords of the first song, a lively, upbeat tune meant to excite the crowd. It was a crowd favorite—fast-paced, energetic, designed to make them feel good, to make them forget about their lives for a while. Lysandra moved across the stage, her movements graceful, fluid, a well-rehearsed dance. The crowd clapped, swayed, and cheered in rhythm.

But as the song reached its peak, something shifted inside her. The music, which had always been a tool of distraction, felt suffocating. The laughter, the applause, the smiles—they felt hollow, like a prison made of sound. She had been here too many times, performing the same scripted act, playing the same role. It was time to break free.

The song ended, and the crowd cheered, waiting eagerly for the next number. Lysandra walked to the center of the stage, the piano awaiting her touch. She stood there for a moment, her heart pounding in her chest. She glanced out at the sea of faces—eager, expectant. She could feel the pull of the system, the weight of expectations pressing down on her. But it wasn't enough to stop her.

She raised the microphone to her lips, her voice soft but carrying across the room.

"I've been thinking," she began, her voice trembling slightly with the weight of the words she was about to say. "I've been thinking about all the songs I've sung for you… all the things I've told you to make you feel safe. But there's something I have to say… something you all need to hear."

The audience quieted, the hushed silence hanging heavy in the air. Lysandra's gaze swept across the room, and for the first time in years, she didn't see the adoring fans. She saw the people—people who had been lulled into complacency by the world's lies.

"This world… this beautiful illusion you think you live in… it's not real. It's all a trap, a game, and you're all playing along without even knowing it," she continued, her voice growing stronger with each word. "You've been given the illusion of freedom, the illusion of choice. But I'm here to tell you the truth… and it will not set you free. No, it will shackle you, imprison you in a way you never imagined."

The room was utterly still. The air seemed thick with confusion, disbelief. Lysandra could feel their eyes on her, the shock, the dissonance. They didn't understand. How could they?

She closed her eyes for a moment, then whispered, "But you'll know. You'll feel it. And when you do, it will be too late."

She turned to the piano and began to play, her fingers light and hesitant at first. Then, the haunting melody began to take shape. It was a song she had never performed before; one she had written in the darkest hours of the night when the weight of the truth became unbearable.

Her voice was soft at first, a whisper that carried the weight of a thousand unspoken words. Each note seemed to tremble with sorrow, with the pain of a world trapped in its own lie.

Whispers in the Dark

The world outside is painted in gold,
But the truth is darker than we're ever told.
We dance in circles, spinning in place,
Chasing shadows, hiding from grace.

Whispers in the dark, they echo so clear,
The truth is out there, but we live in fear.
We cover our ears, we close our eyes,
But the whispers won't fade, they're burning inside.

We build our walls, pretending we're safe,
Living in lies, while our hearts start to break.
We trade our peace for a fleeting high,
And bury the truth we can't deny.

Whispers in the dark, they echo so clear,
The truth is out there, but we live in fear.
We cover our ears, we close our eyes,
But the whispers won't fade, they're burning inside.

The light will fade, the truth will rise,
The whispers will turn to a thunderous cry.

No more running, no more lies,
The world will awaken, or it will die.

Whispers in the dark, no longer unseen,
The silence is breaking, the voices convene.
We stand at the edge, no choice but to see,
The whispers were calling, now they're breaking free.

No more shadows, no more chains,
No more silence to numb the pain.
The whispers were warnings, the whispers were right—
Now they're the chorus that calls in the night.

As the final note rang out, the room was silent—then something extraordinary happened. Slowly, a ripple of movement started, almost imperceptible at first. One person began to clap, unsure but feeling the courage to do so. Then another, and another. Before Lysandra knew it, the applause swelled, like a rising tide of admiration and understanding.

The audience, still reeling from the impact of her words, didn't just clap—they stood. Slowly, one by one, people rose to their feet, clapping harder, faster, in a show of awe, respect, and something deeper—an acknowledgment of her bravery.

Lysandra stood still, her chest tight with emotion as she looked out at the sea of faces, now bright with appreciation. She could see it in their eyes—the understanding, the recognition of the truth she had spoken. They were no longer just fans; they were people who had seen through the veil, just as she had. They had been shaken from the illusion, and in that moment, they knew she was not just a star—she was a messenger.

The applause grew louder, more insistent. The cheers rang through the venue, a cacophony of voices united in admiration, but not for the performance they had expected. No, they were clapping for the woman who had dared to speak the truth. For the artist who had risked everything to expose the lies.

Tears welled up in Lysandra's eyes as she absorbed the moment. For the first time in years, she felt truly seen—not as a symbol, not as an image, but as a person who had shared a piece of her soul with them.

She didn't have the answers. She didn't know what would happen next. But tonight, she had sparked something. And that was all she needed.

The curtain began to fall, but the applause didn't stop. It was a new kind of standing ovation, one rooted in respect and reverence, not for her fame, but for her courage. As the lights dimmed, Lysandra Kaelith smiled—not a practiced smile, but a real one. She had done what she had to do. The rest was up to the world.

CHAPTER 9
EXTINGUISH THE FLAME

The world awoke the next morning to an unexpected and unsettling harmony—a ripple of change that spread across borders, beyond oceans, and through the airwaves. Lysandra Kaelith's performance from the night before was everywhere. The song *Whispers in the Dark* was suddenly the anthem of a collective awakening, its lyrics echoing in the hearts of millions. People across the globe shared it on social media, their posts filled with a mixture of awe, confusion, and curiosity. The once-dismissed whispers of truth now felt urgent, undeniable.

The song was being streamed in record numbers, discussed on every news outlet, and analyzed by scholars, musicians, and conspiracy theorists alike. Forums buzzed with passionate debates—was she a visionary or a madwoman? Some hailed her as a prophet, the voice of a generation ready to unmask the illusions that had kept them enslaved for so long. Others, however, called her a traitor, a dangerous force to be silenced.

But the most significant shift came in the form of the growing movement. Underground groups, once fragmented and disorganized, began to rally around the message Lysandra had broadcasted. Protests began to erupt in cities across the globe, as more people—disillusioned, frightened, but emboldened—questioned the very foundations of their world. For the first time in years, the masses were no longer content to be complacent. They were awakening, slowly but surely.

But in the dark recesses of power, those who had always controlled the strings watched with growing concern.

The black marble chambers of Erebos were cold, but not from the temperature. A tension hung in the air as Emperor Lorkan sat before the Council, his mind weighed down by the unexpected turn of events. The room was dim, lit only by the ethereal glow of floating crystalline lights that seemed to pulse with their own quiet energy.

Lorkan's gaze flickered from the Council members to the holograms that played Lysandra's performance, looping her haunting melody for the hundredth time. The song had gone viral—more than that, it had triggered a spark that seemed to be catching fire everywhere. She was not just another celebrity; she was now the symbol of rebellion.

The Council members murmured uneasily among themselves. Some were frowning, others pacing restlessly, their concerns mounting as they watched the video play out for the hundredth time.

"Her influence is growing," Sythar said, breaking the silence. "We've underestimated her. This... this was never supposed to happen."

Emperor Lorkan's expression remained stoic as he processed the situation. Lysandra was not just a talented performer. She had become a force. A force capable of challenging the foundations they had spent centuries carefully constructing.

Ralyn, his voice low and measured, added, "We should have expected this. She's always been different—too much of an individual. Her words, her music, it was bound to stir something in the masses. But this... This is no longer just a song. It's a movement. And she's leading it."

The holograms flickered, showing scenes from across the world—crowds gathering, protests in the streets, people singing her song. The words "Whispers in the Dark" were everywhere. It was a sensation, an uprising. The song that had once been a cathartic release had now morphed into the anthem of the disillusioned.

The murmurs around the table grew louder, and Lorkan's lips tightened. He knew what had to be done. It was the only way. There could be no room for rebellion, no tolerance for a voice that threatened to expose the fragile illusion they had built.

Finally, he spoke, his voice cutting through the growing unrest of the Council. "We cannot allow this to continue."

The room fell silent.

Lorkan's gaze darkened as he continued. "She is a threat. Her words, her truth, it spreads like wildfire. And if left unchecked, it will grow into something we cannot control. The rebellion, the unrest—it's only the beginning. Soon, it will be more than just protests. It will be chaos. Revolution."

"Then we must act swiftly," Sythar said, his voice grim. "We cannot let this continue. The masses are too easily led, and once the seed of doubt has been planted, it will only grow."

Lorkan's eyes narrowed. "There is only one solution. We eliminate the root of the problem."

The words hung heavy in the air, their finality settling over the Council like a shadow.

The Council members exchanged uneasy glances, but none of them dared to speak against the Emperor's decision. They knew what he meant. Lysandra Kaelith would have to die.

Kosta, who had been quiet up until now, finally shifted in his seat, his eyes narrowing in suspicion. "Assassination? You intend to kill her?"

The tension in the room thickened as the other Council members turned to Kosta. He was young, but he had proven himself in the past with his cunning strategies and quick thinking. Now, his voice was laced with unease.

"We've already discussed all other options," Lorkan replied, his tone icy. "This is not a matter of debate. Lysandra is too dangerous. Her influence will only grow unless we cut it off now. Her death will send a clear message to anyone else who dares to challenge the system we've built."

Kosta leaned forward, his expression conflicted. "But her death—killing her—won't it turn her into a martyr? The people will rally around her. They will make her a symbol of resistance. We risk losing control entirely."

Sythar, his gaze hard, spoke up. "Do you think the people will rally forever, Kosta? They are easily swayed. They crave stability, not revolution. Her death will eliminate the immediate threat, and the people will soon forget. The illusion will hold."

Lorkan's voice was firm. "We have to act decisively. If we allow her to live, we risk her turning into something more—an unstoppable force. Her message is contagious, Kosta. Her death is the only way to contain it before it consumes everything."

Kosta's hands clenched into fists. He knew the weight of Lorkan's words, but the thought of silencing Lysandra for good left him with an uneasy feeling in his gut. "You're certain this is the only way?"

There was a quiet, almost chilling resolve in Lorkan's eyes as he replied, "Yes. Her death is the only way to ensure that the world remains as it is. The Earth, the Erebites—they need the system we've put in place. The stability we provide is necessary. She threatens all of that."

Ralyn nodded. "Her death is for the greater good. It's the only way to preserve order."

The room was silent for a moment as Kosta took in their words. The decision was already made, and no amount of protest would change it.

With a heavy heart, Kosta nodded slowly. "But I still wonder if there's another way."

Lorkan's gaze softened for a moment, but his voice remained firm. "There is no other way."

As the meeting continued, the plans were set into motion. Lysandra Kaelith's time was running out, and the wheels of fate had been set in motion. The illusion they had built would not fall so easily. And if the cost of maintaining that illusion was her life, then so be it.

CHAPTER 10
A SPARK IN THE DARK

The council room remained still, every corner drenched in a haunting silence. Kosta's thoughts churned, replaying the Emperor's cold decree over and over in his mind. His orders were final, and the others had accepted them without question. They saw Lysandra as a threat, a risk that could unravel everything they had worked for, everything the Erebites had built in the shadows of the Earth.

But Kosta felt the weight of the decision as something else—something more personal. He had watched humanity from the hidden depths of his people's domain, a silent observer of a world that had long been manipulated, unaware of the true forces guiding their every move. But Lysandra had shattered that. In one single, defiant act, she had spoken the truth that the Erebites had guarded so fiercely for centuries. Her voice had rippled through society, igniting a spark of awareness, a movement that Kosta wasn't sure his people could control anymore.

The Emperor's voice had been steady, resolute. The decision to eliminate Lysandra was not just a matter of silencing her but preventing the truth she had unearthed from spreading further. The Erebites had long believed that maintaining their power meant keeping the truth hidden. They had thrived on the darkness, manipulating both human history and the course of their world. Lysandra's words had torn down the veil. She had become a beacon of defiance.

But to assassinate her? Kosta clenched his fists, the words echoing in his mind like a drumbeat he couldn't escape. He had hoped for another way—another solution—but now there was only one path laid before him, and it was one he could not walk.

The Emperor's words had sealed her fate, but Kosta couldn't accept them as truth. He had stood by, watching the world shift beneath the surface for too long, but now, Lysandra had awakened something in him that he couldn't ignore. Something had to be done.

He stepped away from the shadowed alcove in the council room, his footsteps echoing in the quiet emptiness. The others had dispersed, their voices hushed as they went about their business, but Kosta's thoughts had not left the room. His mind reeled, searching for a way out of the decision he knew he couldn't accept.

"Why does it have to end like this?" he muttered to himself, pacing the floor, his fingers gripping the edges of the stone table. His thoughts circled, battling between duty and something deeper that refused to be ignored.

His mind returned to her words. Lysandra had spoken not only of truth but of something greater—something the world needed. She had become more than just a threat to the Erebites. She had become a symbol. A symbol that could rally people to believe in something more than the shadows they had lived under for so long.

He paused in front of the tall window that overlooked the dimly lit city below. The lights flickered like tiny stars scattered across a dark expanse, unaware of the storm that was about to break over them. He had grown up in the depths, within the hidden cities of the Erebites, but the surface had always called to him—a world he had only observed from afar. He had always kept his distance, playing his part in maintaining control, keeping humanity in line. But Lysandra had changed that.

"Not like this," Kosta whispered, his voice carrying a resolve he hadn't known he could muster.

Without hesitation, he turned and made his way toward the exit. There would be no more waiting, no more pondering what might have been. The Emperor had made his decision. But Kosta had his own. He would not let them silence her. He would find her, warn her, and give her the chance to escape. If he had to defy his people to protect her, then that's what he would do.

The path ahead was dangerous, but it was one Kosta knew he had to take. His footsteps carried him swiftly through the corridors of the hidden city, the corridors that only the Erebites knew well. As he passed through the ancient stone hallways, his thoughts turned to his next steps.

    The surface was far away. It would take time. But there was no time to waste. He had to move quickly, to reach Lysandra before the Erebites could carry out their plan. He didn't know what would happen when he found her, but one thing was certain—there was no turning back now.

CHAPTER II
SHIFTING THE BALANCE

Days had passed since Lysandra's performance, and her mind was still reeling from the overwhelming reactions to her speech. The applause had been deafening, and the world had responded, but with each passing moment, she couldn't shake the feeling that something darker was approaching. The excitement had faded, leaving behind a gnawing anxiety that grew heavier with each passing hour. Her words had reached the ears of millions, but now she feared that her voice had unwittingly painted a target on her back.

She sat on her couch, lost in thought, when the familiar, oppressive silence of her apartment was broken by a strange sensation. It was as though the air had shifted—subtle but undeniable. Lysandra froze, her breath catching in her throat. She had been on edge for days, but this feeling was different. It was more than just the weight of her own thoughts. Something was approaching.

A soft creak sounded from the door—too soft to be a wind, too deliberate to be an accident. The door swung open without a sound. Lysandra's heart skipped a beat, and she scrambled to her feet, her pulse racing. Standing in the doorway was a man unlike anyone she had ever seen. Tall, impossibly poised, with iridescent skin that shimmered like moonlight on water. His features were sharp, almost regal, as though he were carved from something beyond the realm of human. He seemed to radiate an otherworldly presence, one that filled the room with an intensity she couldn't ignore.

For a moment, Lysandra was paralyzed by the sight of him. She had never seen anyone like this—never even dreamed of such a person. Her heart pounded in her chest as she instinctively took a step back, her breath shallow.

"You're in danger," the stranger said, his voice calm, steady, and without hesitation.

Lysandra's voice caught in her throat. She opened her mouth, but only a breathless whisper came out. "Who... who are you?"

His gaze softened, but there was no mistaking the urgency in his tone. "My name is Kosta. I'm not here to harm you. But your life is in danger. You need to come with me."

Her mind was a blur, but one thing was clear: the fear that had taken root in her chest moments before was now a roaring certainty. The danger she had sensed was real. His appearance, unlike anything she had seen before, seemed to blur the lines between the familiar and something far beyond it. The sleek deep blue and silver garments he wore shimmered in a way that made them feel almost otherworldly. But in the depths of her confusion, there was something else—something inexplicable that made her feel as though she could trust him without understanding why.

"Danger?" she whispered, her voice barely a breath.

"From who?"

"The Erebites," Kosta replied. His eyes locked onto hers with an intensity that felt like it reached into her very soul. "They saw your words as a threat. They want to silence you. If you don't leave now, it will be too late."

Lysandra felt the blood drain from her face. The Erebites? She had heard of them, of course, but only in whispers and rumors. No one dared speak their name openly. And now, apparently, she had become their target. Her own words—her own truth—had made her an enemy. The weight of that knowledge hit her with the force of a wave.

Lysandra hesitated, confusion clouding her thoughts. This man—Kosta—his words rang with conviction, yet nothing about this made sense. Why did he care? But even as questions swirled in her mind, she knew there was no time to ask them. Without further thought, she grabbed her dark red leather coat and followed him out the door.

They moved swiftly through the city streets, Kosta's pace unyielding. Lysandra struggled to keep up, the rapid rhythm of their escape setting her heart pounding in a way that had nothing to do with fear. There was an urgency in his movements that left no room for doubt—this wasn't a mere warning; it was a race against time. Every alleyway, every shadow seemed to hold a secret, and she could feel eyes on her, even though she couldn't see them.

The city seemed unaware of the danger she was in, its lights indifferent to the frantic escape that was unfolding in its midst. Lysandra felt like a stranger here, her feet carrying her away from the world she had known toward an uncertain future. She glanced up at Kosta as they walked, his face unreadable, his movements fluid and deliberate. She had so many questions, but the urgency of the moment kept them at bay.

They eventually reached the outskirts of the city, and Kosta led her into the depths of the forest. The further they went, the more the city's noise and light faded away, swallowed up by the quiet of the trees. There was no turning back now.

After hours of walking, they arrived at a hidden valley—a secluded space untouched by civilization. The air here was different. It felt ancient, as if this place had been waiting for them for centuries. There was a strange, serene stillness to it, the kind of quiet that wrapped around you like a blanket and made the rest of the world seem distant, almost irrelevant.

"This place," Kosta said, his voice steady and calm, "is where you'll be safe. Not even the Erebites can trace us here."

Lysandra's eyes scanned the valley, taking in the untouched landscape. The trees stood tall and proud, their branches swaying in the wind, and the air felt crisp and pure. It was as if she had stepped into another world—a world far removed from the chaos and danger she had left behind. She felt an odd sense of peace here, but also an overwhelming sense of isolation. For the first time, she felt the full weight of her situation. She was truly alone.

"Why are you helping me?" Lysandra's voice broke the silence, steady but uncertain. "Who are you?"

Kosta stood still for a moment, eyes distant, as if weighing the right words. When he finally spoke, it was with an unhurried confidence. "My people have lived hidden beneath the Earth for longer than most can imagine. We've watched humanity, guided them through the shadows, protected them when needed. But now... now everything is shifting. You've seen what was meant to remain unseen. You've become a danger to them."

Lysandra's brow furrowed. "Why me? What makes me so important?"

Kosta turned to her, his gaze piercing. "Because you've glimpsed the truth. Not just seen it—you've torn back their veil. You are the key to everything they've worked to hide, and you've become a symbol of their greatest fear. A symbol of rebellion."

Her mind raced. She had always known her words carried power, but this? She hadn't understood how deep her actions reached until now. She wasn't just a threat—she was a beacon, one they couldn't let stand.

"What happens now?" The question escaped her in a breathless whisper, though the answer felt like a weight she wasn't sure she could bear.

Kosta's expression softened, but his eyes remained firm. "Now, we take a moment to breathe. We assess what's next. I believe you hold the power to change the world, Lysandra, but we have to tread carefully. The Erebites will stop at nothing to silence you."

Lysandra nodded slowly, absorbing the weight of his words. *The power to change the world?* What was Kosta talking about? Either way, there was no going back now. The choice she had made was irreversible, and the path ahead was uncertain at best.

As the silence settled over them, the air cool against her skin, Lysandra couldn't help but study Kosta. It wasn't just the strangeness of him—there was something about the steadiness he exuded, an unwavering calm in the face of danger. She realized, for the first time in what felt like forever, that she didn't have to face this alone. Whatever came next, they would face it together.

CHAPTER 12
THROUGH ENEMY GATES

The night felt like it was holding its breath. The stars shimmered above in a crystal-clear sky, but their light did little to calm Lysandra's restless mind. She could feel the hum of tension in the stillness—the calm before the storm.

Lysandra stared up at the darkened sky, the weight of the universe pressing down on her chest. She had always been a woman who spoke her truth, but now, her truth had put her in the crosshairs of forces far beyond her understanding.

Kosta sat across from her, his gaze distant as though searching for answers in the starlit expanse. Finally, his voice broke the silence, low and steady, but full of an undeniable resolve.

"We can't hide forever, Lysandra," he said, his breath visible in the cold night air, coming out in soft, misty clouds.

"The longer we stay here, the closer they get. They're watching. And we will run out of places to hide. We need to go to Erebos and reason with them."

She shivered—not from the cold, but from the certainty in his words. Every fiber of her being screamed to stay hidden, to run away. Yet, Kosta's determination rooted her to the spot. The only way to escape would be to disappear entirely, and even that wasn't certain. The Erebites would hunt them down, and it would only be a matter of time before the walls closed in.

"I'm not ready," Lysandra whispered, her voice barely audible against the wind. She felt small under the weight of it all.

"You don't need to be ready," Kosta replied with a quiet intensity, his eyes meeting hers. The faintest glimmer of starlight reflected in his iridescent skin, giving him an almost ethereal quality. "You just need to be strong."

Lysandra hesitated, the magnitude of his words sinking in like stones thrown into a dark lake.

"Okay. Let's go", she finally said, with as much confidence as she could muster.

They would go to Erebos, the heart of the Erebites' domain, and face whatever awaited them.

Kosta nodded and extended his hand, his fingertips tingling as raw energy coiled around them like a living current. A luminous orb took shape in the air before him, its glow undulating with an almost sentient pulse. The atmosphere shifted, growing dense with unseen forces that crackled and swirled, distorting the very space around them.

"Hold on," he warned, gripping Lysandra's wrist.

The orb surged outward, wrapping around them like a living entity, its surface shimmering with ethereal energy. Before Lysandra could understand what was happening, she was flying to the city of Erebos, encapsulated by light. Not flying in the air but flying through tunnels carved into the Earth ages ago by the Erebites.

The city of Erebos was a world unlike any Lysandra had ever known. The city's gates gleamed with light, pulsing in rhythmic patterns like the beating of a divine heart. Erebos was a city of stunning beauty and otherworldly technology—an architectural marvel bathed in perpetual light. Towers of shimmering materials stretched impossibly high, their surfaces glinting like polished gems, casting their ethereal glow into the boundless expanse above.

As they approached the gates, two tall Erebite soldiers stood motionless, their armor gleaming like polished metal, reflecting the city's light in a way that made them appear almost otherworldly. Their faces were hidden beneath gleaming visors, their expressions unreadable but undeniably present.

Kosta stepped forward, his movements fluid and deliberate, as though he had been here many times before. The guards barely moved, their cold eyes fixed on him, sizing him up. The air hummed with tension as they exchanged a wordless glance before stepping aside.

"Follow us," one of the soldiers muttered, his voice flat, devoid of emotion.

The corridors of Erebos felt alive with the pulse of energy, the walls lined with light-drenched stone and sleek, glowing technology. The citizens they passed were not vacant, but focused—moving with purpose, their expressions calm, absorbed in their own thoughts. There was a serenity in the city that Lysandra couldn't ignore, a sense of control and balance that seemed to permeate every corner.

They arrived at the heart of the city: a grand hall unlike any other. The space was vast, its vaulted ceilings stretching endlessly upward, filled with swirling light patterns that seemed to dance through the air. The architecture was divine in its proportions, grand columns of light-infused material rising from the floor, their edges glowing softly in the warm light of the room.

At the center of the room stood Emperor Lorkan. His presence was overwhelming, like the darkness of a stormcloud before it unleashed its fury. His black cloak trailed behind him like liquid night, and his eyes, sharp and calculating, locked onto Kosta the moment they entered. Every step he took seemed to command the air itself.

Lorkan's gaze was heavy as he spoke, his voice deep, as rich and unforgiving as the stone that surrounded them. "You've made quite a mess of things, my son," he said, his tone filled with cold disappointment. "You were one of our most trusted, and yet you chose to betray us."

Kosta didn't flinch. His stance was unyielding, his gaze never wavering from Lorkan's. "I didn't betray you, Emperor. I did what I believed was right."

Lysandra's breath hitched in her throat. *My son?* She didn't know how to process the words. Kosta is the son of the Emperor? The realization struck her like a bolt of lightning, so sudden and forceful that it left her momentarily stunned. She had always sensed there was something deeper about Kosta, some connection he wasn't revealing. But this? This was unimaginable.

Her eyes darted between the two men, Kosta's defiance and Emperor Lorkan's cold authority, and the weight of the moment hit her with brutal force. Kosta, the man she had trusted, was the son of the very ruler she had despised. The revelation sent her mind spinning, pieces of half-formed thoughts colliding without finding their place.

The more she tried to make sense of him, the less she understood. His strength, his quiet intensity—they'd always seemed out of place, like pieces of a puzzle that didn't quite fit. But now, with this revelation, the pieces began to shift, and something much bigger emerged. This wasn't just about protecting her; it was something tied to the heart of the Erebite empire, and she was nowhere near ready to understand what that truly meant.

Lysandra's mind raced as the weight of the revelation began to settle on her shoulders. She tried to steady her breath, but the air felt thin and foreign, and the ground beneath her feet suddenly seemed less solid.

Lorkan's eyes darkened, his expression a tight mask of displeasure. The air in the room seemed to grow heavier, the silence pressing in on Lysandra's chest.

Before Kosta could say another word, the guards stepped forward. "Take them to separate holding areas," Lorkan commanded, his voice thick with finality. "We'll have the hearing tomorrow. For now, they need rest."

CHAPTER 13
THROUGH THEIR EYES

The following day, the council chamber was no less imposing. The room, vast and awe-inspiring, was bathed in light that cascaded from high-embedded panels in the ceiling, casting radiant patterns across the polished stone floors. The walls, crafted from an iridescent material, shimmered with every movement, reflecting the room's glow in a way that made the entire space feel alive. It was not a place meant to intimidate, but to awe, a testament to the immense power that the Erebites commanded over both technology and the forces of light.

Seated on their elevated thrones, the council members looked like figures carved from stone—severe, stoic, and perfectly composed. Their faces were unreadable, their expressions a mask of calm authority that spoke of centuries of power. Lysandra and Kosta stood below them, the weight of the council's judgment heavy upon them, while the subtle hum of the room seemed to grow louder, as if the very air was attuned to their presence.

At the head of the room, Lorkan stood like a force of nature. His posture was commanding, and his gaze sharp as ever. He wasn't just the ruler of this space; he was its embodiment. Though his eyes initially found Kosta's, it was Lysandra who felt the full measure of his focus. He seemed to envelop the entire room with his presence, as if he were both distant and all-encompassing, his power radiating outwards and commanding everything it touched.

"Let us begin," Lorkan's voice was low, his words heavy with authority. "Kosta, you are charged with treason. You aided Lysandra in spreading her dangerous message, in defying the order of the Erebites. You chose to protect her at the expense of the Erebite system."

Kosta stood tall, his back straight, his voice unwavering. "I did not betray the Erebites," he said, his tone calm yet forceful. "I saw a way forward that didn't involve silencing her. I saw a way where we could have explained the necessity of our actions to her. She could have become an ally, not an enemy."

Lysandra's heart twisted with conflict as she listened. Kosta's words resonated with a part of her that wanted to believe in a future where the Erebites weren't simply tyrants. She wanted to understand his perspective. Could it be that there was another way?

She turned her gaze sharply to Kosta, her words cutting through the tension. "Why would I ever help them?" she demanded, her voice trembling with a mix of frustration and disbelief. "Everything I've uncovered shows the Erebites for what they are—manipulators, controlling every inch of life. They have taken are freedom, and have left us with only the illusion of freedom."

Lorkan's gaze hardened as he fixed his eyes on Lysandra. The silence in the council chamber felt like it could crush her, his presence commanding the room with an iron grip. The cold stone walls around them seemed to close in, amplifying his every word.

"You misunderstand," Lorkan said, his voice sharp and unwavering. "The truth you speak—your vision of a world where humanity is free from our control—does not exist. A world without us is a world on the edge of collapse."

Lysandra's eyes burned with defiance. "Collapse? You speak of stability, but what about the wars? The suffering? You allowed countries to rise and fall, fueling conflict for centuries. How many have died in your pursuit of control?"

Lorkan's expression did not waver. "And do you believe war would cease in our absence?" he asked, his voice almost gentle. "Do you believe that if we had not guided humanity, they would have simply found peace on their own?"

Lysandra hesitated. "You fostered division. You created ideologies and let people kill in their names."

Lorkan nodded slowly. "We allowed humanity to fight battles they were already destined to fight. The wars you condemn were not our doing; they were humanity's nature."

His gaze bore into hers. "We always made sure humanity never destroyed itself and the Earth. Knowing that war is inevitable, we chose to orchestrate them to benefit humanity overall. Consider this. War is not merely destruction. It is the fire that tempers the blade, the struggle that forces humanity to grow. Without conflict, there is no progress. Without challenge, there is no strength."

Lysandra felt the weight of his words press down on her. She wanted to refute them, to reject the idea that war was inevitable, but something in his voice made her pause. Had they only channeled the chaos into something survivable?

"You claim we nurtured war," Lorkan continued, "but consider this—without our hand in shaping the conflicts of the past, where would humanity be19. today?"

Lysandra clenched her fists, her mind a storm of doubt and conviction. She had come here believing in a truth, but now she wasn't sure if the truth had ever been hers to hold. The silence in the council chamber deepened, the weight of history pressing in around her.

For the first time, she wasn't sure what to say.

"You've seen our influence. The laws we enforce keep order. The structures we've built allow for trade, for the exchange of knowledge. The entire world depends on the delicate balance we maintain. Without us, the infrastructure we've created would dissolve into rubble. And when that happens, humanity will not recover," Lorkan pressed, his voice lowering, carrying the weight of finality. "It would be every man, woman, and child for themselves. And the strong would rise to crush the weak. The weak would either perish or fight back in futile attempts to survive, spiraling into endless cycles of bloodshed."

Lysandra shuddered at the thought, her chest tight. She had always believed in the power of the individual, in the potential of human beings to create a fair world. But this... this was not a world where fairness could survive. She could see the cracks in the illusion she had held onto, but the question still lingered: Did it have to be this way?

"And the Erebites—" Lorkan continued, his voice steady and calm, though there was an unmistakable fire in his eyes. "We do not seek power for its own sake. We do not wish to rule out of desire for domination. We do it to protect you. To ensure that humanity can survive in a world filled with threats far beyond its understanding. We keep the chaos at bay, and we have done so for millennia."

Lysandra's mind spun as Lorkan's words hit her like a storm, each one leaving her more confused than the last. The weight of her truth, the burden of what she had uncovered, suddenly felt too heavy to carry. She wanted to believe in the world she had imagined, one where everyone was free, but the fear in her chest, the fear of a world without this control, began to take root.

Lorkan continued, his voice dipping into a lower register, rich with authority. "Without the guidance of the Erebites, the chaos would bleed into every corner of the world. Those who seek power would destroy everything we've built. Take a look at the cities—look at the technology, the infrastructure. The Erebites gave humanity the means to survive. Without us, there would be no knowledge, no security, no trade. There would be no future."

His words reverberated in the air as Lysandra felt the world around her grow heavy. Was it truly possible? Could humanity really not survive without the Erebites? She had always wanted a future where the world could choose its own path, but Lorkan's depiction of a world without that control felt suffocating.

"You call us tyrants," Lorkan continued, his voice cutting through the tension, "but we are the foundation upon which everything else is built. Without us, the world would collapse. We give the people something they cannot give themselves: Purpose. Progress. Perseverance."

The words stung, each one like a lash against the vision she had fought for. The world she wanted to see—one of freedom, of choice, of balance—felt impossible now. She opened her mouth to speak, but the words caught in her throat. Could she argue against his logic?

"I never wanted to destroy," Lysandra managed to whisper, her voice hoarse. "But you've controlled us. You've kept us in the dark about what's really happening."

Lorkan's eyes softened slightly, but his voice remained firm. "The Erebites are not the enemy, Lysandra. We never have been. We've kept the world intact. We've preserved humanity from itself. And now, we give you a choice: accept what Kosta has suggested—become our ally, accept the guidance we give, and together we will continue to build this world."

Lysandra felt the crushing weight of his words settle deep within her chest, each syllable an anchor pulling her further down. She had come to Erebos without knowing what to expect, but the reality unfolding before her left her breathless. Was it possible that the Erebites' control was truly necessary for survival? Had she been blind to the complexity of the world she had been trying to change?

Her heart hammered in her chest as the council room sank into a heavy silence. The flickering light cast long, wavering shadows on the stone walls, intensifying the pressure of the decision before her. She stood at a crossroads—a path leading to everything she had fought for, and another that beckoned with a truth she didn't fully understand, but couldn't deny.

Made in the USA
Columbia, SC
20 March 2025

be400a4c-6b81-4f10-81c6-6120c0252866R01